For Jenny ~ JC
For Lola ~ CF

African elephants are the world's largest land mammals.
They are twice as tall as and fifty times heavier than a man. Their front teeth have grown
into tusks and their noses into trunks – the longest noses in the world!
These gentle giants are incredibly intelligent and, like people, can live for sixty to seventy years.
Male elephants leave home when they are teenagers, but females stay at home with their
mothers and the rest of the family for their entire lives. Herds are led by the oldest
and most experienced female, who is known as the matriarch. When baby elephants get upset
or angry, their mothers and the other older females in the herd – known as their aunties –
calm them down and make sure they feel safe and behave themselves.

Care for the Wild International is an animal welfare and conservation charity committed
to protecting African elephants in the wild and rehabilitating sick or injured orphans.
To find out more about elephants, or to adopt an elephant like little Trumpet,
simply visit www.careforthewild.com or write to
CWI, The Granary, Tickfold Farm, Kingsfold, West Sussex, RH12 3SE.

SIMON AND SCHUSTER
First published in Great Britain in 2006 by Simon & Schuster UK Ltd
Africa House, 64-78 Kingsway, London WC2B 6AH
A CBS COMPANY

Text copyright © 2006 Jane Clarke
Illustrations copyright © 2006 Charles Fuge
The right of Jane Clarke and Charles Fuge to be identified as the author
and illustrator of this work has been asserted by them in accordance
with the Copyright, Designs and Patents Act, 1988

Book designed by Genevieve Webster
The text for this book is set in Garamond
The illustrations are rendered in watercolour

A CIP catalogue record for this book is available from
the British Library upon request

ISBN 1 416 90481 6
EAN 9781416904816
Printed in China
1 3 5 7 9 10 8 6 4 2

TRUMPET

The Little
Elephant
with a **BIG**
Temper

Jane Clarke & Charles Fuge

SIMON AND SCHUSTER
London New York Sydney

It was Trumpet's birthday.

Mrs Trumpeter was finishing his cake.

Trumpet and his sister were building mud towers.

"My tower's better than yours," boasted Tilly.

"But mine has to be the best!" Trumpet said. "It's my birthday!"

He plopped a glob of mud on top of his tower,

then another, and another.

The tower wobbled . . .

It toppled to the ground. SPLAT!
Trumpet's ears flared.
He swayed from side to side, swinging his trunk.
"Haroomph!" he trumpeted,
trampling all over the toppled tower.

"Calm down, Trumpet!" said Tilly.

"Oh, Trumpet!" said Mrs Trumpeter.
"You must calm down,
or you'll spoil your birthday party."
So Trumpet rolled round in the cool mud.
"I'm better now, Mummy," he said at last.
"Well done!" said his mother.
"Let's have lunch!"

The juiciest leaves were
high above Trumpet's head.
Trumpet stood on tiptoe, and
str-e-e-e-tched out his trunk.
He grasped the tip
of a leaf and pulled.

B-O-O-O-ING!

The leaf and the branch
twanged out of Trumpet's reach.
His ears flared.
He began to sway from
side to side . . .

"Calm down, Trumpet!"
warned Mrs Trumpeter.
"You'll spoil your party!"

But it was no good.

"Haroomph!" Trumpet trumpeted,
stomping so hard that all the dead leaves
fell off the tree. The dry leaves and dust swirled
and whirled as Trumpet swung his trunk.
"Count to ten with me!" coughed Mrs Trumpeter.
"1...2...3...4...5...6...7...8...9...10!"

"I'm better now, Mummy," Trumpet said.
"That's my Trumpet," said his mother. "Next time,
try counting to ten before you lose your temper.
Now, let's get down to the waterhole.

It's partytime!"

Tail in trunk, they made their way to the waterhole.

Mrs Trumpeter carefully set down the cake.
"Yummy! Bananas and peanuts –
my favourites! It's the best birthday
cake ever!" Trumpet squealed.
"I'm glad you like it," his mother said.
"It took me ages to make!"

"Look, Mummy!"

Trumpet's tail twitched with excitement.
"My friends are here. Time for cake!"
"After the games," his mother smiled.

The games were great fun. Beryl won Bush Bash.

Percy and Pansy won Pick a Peanut.

Winston won Push of War.

The next game was Dead Lions.

"It's my birthday!" said Trumpet. "I want to win!"

They lay as still as stones.

A bee landed on Percy's nose. Pansy giggled as Percy squealed.

"You're out!" said Mrs Trumpeter.

The bee settled on Winston's horn. He snorted hard.

"You're out!" said Mrs Trumpeter.

The bee buzzed round Tilly. Tilly's tail twitched,
    but Mrs Trumpeter didn't see. Tilly's tail tickled Beryl's nose.

"AAATISHOOOO!"

Beryl sneezed. Trumpet jumped.

"You're out!" said Mrs Trumpeter.

"It's not fair!" Trumpet wailed. "It's my birthday!"
Tears of rage spurted from his eyes.
"Here we go again," muttered Tilly.

"I have to calm down!" Trumpet thought.
So he took a deep breath and counted:

"1...2...3...4...5...6...7...8...9...10!"
And, sure enough, it worked! He felt calm again.
"Is it cake time yet?" he asked, wiping
his eyes with his trunk.
"Almost," said Mrs Trumpeter,
giving him a hug.

"Why don't you all play Squirt the Dirt first?"
"Yippee!"
They hurtled towards the waterhole.

SPLOSH!

They came up spluttering,
and began to squirt and splash each other.

"Mind the cake!"

Mrs Trumpeter shouted. "It took ages to make!"

Too late.

SQUELCH!

"My cake!" shrieked Trumpet and Mrs Trumpeter together.
The cake was demolished by the deluge.
"Uh-oh . . ." said Tilly.

Mrs Trumpeter's ears flared.
Tears of rage sprang to her eyes.
She swayed from side to side,
swinging her trunk.
"HAROOMPH!"
she trumpeted.
Mrs Trumpeter was quivering from
the tips of her tusks to the
end of her tufty tail.

Everyone hid behind the termite mound.

"Calm down, Mummy!" Trumpet yelled.

But Mrs Trumpeter was too cross to hear one little elephant.

"Help me!" Trumpet said. "Everyone count to ten as loud as you can!"

"1...2...3...4...5...6...7...8...9...10!"

"That's better!" said Mrs Trumpeter, sitting
on the termite mound and flattening it.
"Well done, Mummy," said Trumpet. "You're nice and
calm now. You haven't spoilt the party."

"But what about the cake?" Mrs Trumpeter asked.

"Let's eat it!" Trumpet said. "We'll do a cake countdown!"

"10...9...8...7...6...5...4...3...2...1!"
they counted. Then they guzzled up the gooey cake.

"It's yummy, Mummy," Trumpet said.

"YUMMY!" everyone agreed, and they all sang
"Happy Birthday, dear Trumpet" as loudly as they could.
Trumpet looked round at the sticky, smiling faces.

"It's the best birthday ever!" he beamed.